Shocking Experiments at Paradise Cove

By David Evans

Table of Contents

Chapter 1 It Begins 5

Chapter 2 Catastrophe 17

Chapter 3 What's Next 29

Chapter 4 Deterioration 42

Chapter 5 Observations 53

Chapter 6 Thoughts 63

Chapter 7 Fierce Battle 75

It was the year 2033, and there were many experiments being conducted at paradise cove. No one is allowed, to swim in the cove for safety reasons.

The cove is no longer as pretty as it used to be, for the water, now is a blackish color. But the water used to be so clear that you didn't even know you were in the water.

The water is a precise seventy-five degrees. The experiments that have occurred are top secret and aren't disclosed with the general public. There are seven scientists that worked at the cove. Each scientist had their own set of skills. Their main study was biology and marine reptiles, and sharks.

Half of the facility is beneath the surface of paradise cove. The cove is two hundred feet deep. Coves are usually just a few feet deep but this cove is special in those regards. The cove was constructed like a large, oversized swimming pool. At the bottom of the cove is sand and a real reef that was brought in from Australia.

Some of the experiments are extremely dangerous and for this reason there are four armed guards that patrol the perimeter on a daily basis.

The armed guards aren't too friendly and like to be left alone and not talked to. Each armed guard is given an M16 and a side arm and one grenade.

None of the armed guards have had to use their weapons even once and that's a good thing. Just the other day the Pentagon, sent a message to the president about the new experiments that the army wants to be held at paradise cove.

Chapter 1: It Begins

The Pentagon has just funded the experiments at the cove to go on for another year. After the Pentagon was thinking about closing down the lab and laying off the workers. Unless they make more progress on their four new experiments.

So far one of their experiments has been going well and the Pentagon is very pleased with the progress. This project consists of dolphins being taught how to read and do sneak attacks on military vessels.

The dolphins will have to go through some strength training to see if they can hold bombs on their flippers.

None of the three dolphins that went through the test were harmed. The one dolphins name is Mr. Blue, he's the largest out of the two other dolphins. The other dolphins are female and are smaller than Mr. Blue. These dolphins are given treats after they progress on through their training.

It took Mr. blue three days just to learn one word in English, the word was stop. The scientists were so proud of him that they set him free after they were done experimenting on him. However, they weren't allowed to let him back into the main ocean.

He set him free in a big part of their lab to enjoy the remaining years of his life. Mr. blue was very strong and could easily leap up out of the water and do a back flip all at the same time. He could hold even the largest of bombs on his left side. They would load him up and think that the weight would stop him but it never did. He would just keep on going and going, it seemed like he was unstoppable in some instances.

He had experimental mini missile launchers on his both flippers. The missile launching system was hard wired in his brain.

The wires then couldn't have been removed. However, the wires didn't seem to bother him and he would just keep on swimming. This whole program cost the Pentagon three million dollars.

The scientists didn't like to have put the wires in Mr. Blues brain but it was what they were instructed to do.

It took them three hours to get all the wires into his brain and set up the wires to the main bomb. If the dolphins couldn't finish its mission while out in the field it was having to blow itself up. This was sad but the government didn't want anyone else to get ahold of the wires and the dolphin.

Mr. Blue is no longer going to be used in combat, he was just an experiment that went well. But another one of the experiments didn't go so well. One day Mr. Blue escaped his enclosure and swam away into the open ocean.

He swam for a while and soon came upon another dolphin, that wasn't very happy about his presence there. He swam away from that dolphin and went hunting for something to eat. He happened to look up at the surface of the water, there was a sea turtle.

His one flipper was caught in a zip lock baggie, causing him to swim erratically. He very carefully approached him and went over to his flipper. He closed his mouth on the turtles flipper pulling the baggie off of it.

The turtle then quickly swam off, the dolphin swam over to the reef. There were schools of fish swimming around, among a few barracudas. The barracudas were eyeing up their prey, while circling the reef.

Eventually the dolphin found his pod and felt well once again. The second project was called the moray eel project, they had four moray eels. They didn't really name them, but just named them numbers.

The moray eels weren't treated very kindly and this caused one of them to die from being mishandled and beaten up. The one scientist didn't like eels and would take his anger out on the poor eels.

The four eels were special in their own ways. They were all the same size and would bite so when handling them the scientist would have to wear welding gloves.

The 3rd project was called the Jellyfish project, where they studied the many types of jellyfish. What they found to be interesting was how one of the species of newly discovered jellyfish was able to generate a shock, similar to that of an electric eel. It also glows in the dark, because of its bioluminescence.

Some of the jellyfish's tentacles glow blue, while the rest of its tentacles are see through. This Jellyfish was named shock and glow, this jellyfish species lives for a hundred years.

Most jellyfish species live between 12-18 months before dying and evaporating. There are over 200 species of jellyfish that are found all over the world.

The immortal jellyfish has been said to be able to live on forever, it's said that it'll regenerate and restart its life cycle.

The 4th project is called the salamanders project, this was the most horrific project done so far. They had 20 salamanders living in several aquariums, they were handled many times throughout a day.

They were injected with cells from a Komodo dragon, and muscle cells from the frilled lizard. After they were all injected, they were given several hours to rest. The scientists noticed that they were more aggressive, when going after their prey.

The scientists checked their mouths to see if they grown any teeth but they didn't. Next they mixed some compounds together and injected it into them.

They were positive that the compound, would increase their agility and would make their bodies produce cells that would cure certain conditions. Just a day later one of them died, not knowing what to do one of the scientists tazed it.

It woke up for a short while, but shortly after died. Just a few hours later the salamanders bodies changed to a purple color and they died. They were buried 40 feet away from the facility on dry land.

Little did they know what they would turn into. The scientists were sad and couldn't get over the deaths of the salamanders, we shouldn't have given them those final injections. If we wouldn't have, then our superiors would have fired us.

You could have just thrown away the compound, and the needles. You wouldn't have gotten away with that, there are cameras watching us from every angle. It's time that we get over it, our whining isn't going to bring them back.

We really should get back to our tasks, we need to complete our observations of the jellyfish's. I think that there awfully boring to watch, especially the one that I think never moves.

I measured the distance that it traveled, it moved slightly. I had my hand too close to the shocking jellyfish, it felt threatened and shocked me.

> "How many times in a day do you think it can produce a shock?"

> "5 times."

Now I'm going to quiz you, I wasn't ready for no quiz.

> "How many tentacles do they have?"

> "4-8."

> "Do they have brains, hearts, or eyes?"

> "No," they don't have brains, hearts, or eyes.

> "What's the largest species of jellyfish?"

> "The Lion's mane jellyfish."

"What's the most domestic breed of jellyfish?"

"The moon jellyfish."

That finishes up all of my questions, I'm glad that you're done so soon. We've been having the same thing for lunch for so long, we should go get some Italian food.

Our boss has been awfully quiet today, you should be happy for that. The last time that he was talkative, he had me do 2 projects in one day. That doesn't sound too bad to me, then I'll have him give you some more projects to do.

Chapter 2: Catastrophe

You see these stack of papers, I was up to one in the morning working on these. Now I think you're making it up, then the room grew silent. After that, they all got back to work.

The one scientist was a tall fellow with long fingers and had an annoying laugh. He has premature balding and was told by his Dr. that he was going to lose all of his that next month, which in the end set him off and put him in a sour mood for the rest of the month.

He likes to research things on his own and doesn't like to share his findings with his colleagues.

He works all day at the lab in paradise cove and actually lives on the cove in the lab apartment. All the other scientists don't live on the campus.

The other scientists have to drive an hour just to get to the laboratory each day. The rule is everyone has to sign in and log what they did for the day and if they don't they're fired.

Last week the oldest scientist on campus fell asleep while driving to the lab and crashed into a barn.

This caused him to be late getting to the lab, he works too many long hours and hasn't been sleeping very well at night. His kids are always worrying about him, his kids say that he's a workaholic.

However, he wasn't injured that bad. He crashed his old pickup truck and hit his head on the steering wheel. His truck started up again and he was back on his way.

He knew that it was not right to leave the old barn all cracked up and didn't wait for the owner of the barn to show up.

All he cared about was his job because it was his life's priority. However today was a Wednesday and he didn't feel like signing in and forgot to sign in and didn't write down what he did that day.

He was supposed to be working with the Moray eels but decided to sit down in the desk chair and fell asleep.

He fell asleep and was sleeping for two hours until the labs boss showed up an hour later and came up behind him and tapped him on the shoulder. Look you're going to have to get up or else.

I mean you better wake up now or I'll fire you and give you a ten dollar fine not signing in. I'm going to give you just one more warning then you're out of here, I don't care what you have to say about it. Damon opened his eyes and began to laugh to himself.

"What's so funny?"

"You're so funny"

I don't even think you're doing your job the way you should be. Be quiet, you have no room to talk here and you know it.

"Are you going to read me my rights?"

"No," and look you're getting on my nerves.

You're incompetent and are now fired, what do you think about that. You know what Mr. Pike I should punch you in the face and walk out of this pathetic place.

I've been working here for five years and now I'm fired. Damon walked over to his desk and looked down at it. You know Mr. Pike all these papers that you see her piled up on my desk were made and researches by me.

Now all I can do is throw them in the trash and go home and be depressed and get drunk. I didn't know that you were a drunk.

Drunks aren't allowed to work here, and yeah Mr. Pike I lied when I signed up for the job. I lied and said I wasn't a drunk. You sneaky little snake you, I should have known that you were a drunk.

My favorite kind of liquor is whiskey, I have a flask in the middle console of my truck. The flask is full of whiskey.

> "Who do you think you are?"

> "I'm just doing my job; I've heard enough of you ranting and raving on about why you shouldn't be fired."

My boss would fire me too if I didn't do my job. So come on, give me your card and key and I'm going to walk you out. Damon picked up a stack of papers and threw it at Mr. Pike.

You're acting like a little baby that's getting his way, I can't believe you threw all those papers at me.

You think that's going to help, you're still fired and after today. I don't want to see your face again, if I do I'll turn away, I can't stand living like this.

I don't sleep not even a wink and now I come to work and you fire me. I'm done and that's it, no you're not now you're coming with me, okay then I will if I must.

"What are you thinking?"

"I'm thinking that I'll jump into the eel pool and let them shock me to death"

"How would that make you feel?"

"It would break my heart to see you take your own life like that, you still have a long life ahead of you and no you won't be receiving retirement from the lab either or from me."

"Are you going to stop me from jumping in the eel pool?"

"Mr. Pike grabbed Damon by his left arm." Oh, you don't want me to commit suicide.

"No," I don't that would be just horrific.

"You have no regards for me do you?"

"Yes," I do and I care about you.

I bet you don't like me working here. You're right I didn't like you working here, you make me very nervous especially when you handle the eels.

Oh, I handle them with great care, then explain to me why of the eels died last week. He was an old dumb eel anyway.

Hey, don't even think about pushing me, I'll push back on you and you might lose your balance. Oh, stop worrying about me. I don't appreciate you pushing me if I slip and fall in the electric eel pool.

I'm going to pull you down with me, I'm in no mood to deal with you and I'm not afraid to handcuff you. You talk so big, but I don't see you doing much of anything.

I can't there's limited room between you and me, I don't want either one of us falling into the shocking eel pool.

Suddenly Damon slipped and Mr. Pike was no longer holding onto him and he fell down twenty feet into the electric eel pool.

He yelled out help me, please do something, what do you want me to do. I can feel the eels swimming around me, don't move and they'll leave you alone.

> "Why can't you throw a rope down to me?"

> "The eels are biting me, please do something or I'm going to die."

I don't want you to die on me. Another eel bit me, please do something more than just staring at me.

> "Why do you think I'm trying to do?"

> "I'm trying to help you out and you just want to keep shouting at me."

I'm shouting because I'm so scared and don't want to die today. I can't find a rope; I have looked everywhere. I'll be right back, no please don't go I need you. I'm going to call for help.

I should be back in five minutes. No, you don't have five minutes. Mr. Pike walked down the hallway and looked for someone to help him. It seemed like everyone was busy, Mr. Pike didn't feel like, disturbing any of his workers.

Chapter 3: What's Next

He thought to himself I hope that I can find someone to help. He looked in the one lab room and saw that there was a young man sitting at a desk studying his papers.

He knocked on the lab door once and the guy still didn't even get up to see who was knocking at the door.

Damon looked closer and saw that his ear buds were in his ears and he probably couldn't even hear him knock.

He knocked again and this time he really wrapped on the door. That seemed to get his attention, he stood up and looked over at Mr. Pike.

Mr. Pike waved his arms and yelled I need your help right now. The young man came to the door and opened it.

"What's your name?"

"My name is Daten."

"I'm having an emergency here, what kind of emergency?"

"Damon fell into the electric eel pool and I can't get him out."

Walk with me to the eel pool.

"Do you know where there would be some rope?"

"No," I don't

"How are you going to help me?"

"I can help you to make a plan to extract him from the eel pool."

"No," I need you to help me to get him out now.

I don't know how I'm going to help, but I'll try. They walked into the room and saw that Damon was floating on the surface of the water face down. I think that he's dead.

There's blood in the water, his one foot appears to be missing. I think that the electric eels are eating him, you know it's my fault for his death.

"How did he fall in there in the first place?"

"He must have slipped and fell, he was arguing with me and tried to push me into the eel pool."

"Why did he try to push you into the eel pool?"

"Because I fired him"

"Why did you fire him?"

He mistreated an eel and let it die and didn't even care. He was also late to work and refused to write down what he had done today. That was wrong of him.

"How do you plan on getting the dead body out of the eel pool?"

"I don't know yet?"

"Did you log what happened here?"

"No," I didn't

"I have something to tell you"

"What is it?"

"We're having some security problems."

"Okay what is going on?"

"There's a hippy that lives a few miles from here and used to work here many years ago."

Yesterday he drove up to the gate in his Beatle bus. When the security guard told him he wasn't allowed to come in, he went crazy and was swearing at him and tried to punch him.

Then after his crazy attack, he said that he wanted to come in and take the eels and save them.

He's obsessed with eels and all must of went out of mind and all he can talk about are eels. The security guard also told me that this man is homeless and doesn't care about his looks.

"How many times has he tried to get in?"

"He has tried twice this week to get in."

"Does he have any weapons?"

"Yes," apparently he has a baton and pellet gun.

"Has he tried to shoot the security guard?"

"Yes."

he shot him in the arm with the pellet gun but was able to get the pellet gun away from him. Then he got out of his bus and tried to beat the officer with his baton, the officer forced him down to the ground and placed handcuffs around his hands.

The very next day the man came back and tried to get in again. But this time the security officer was ready for him. He told the man to get away from the gate, he didn't listen to him.

He said to the man I'll tell you twice then I'll take you down. The guy's eyes got as big as saucers, he backed up his bus and drove away.

"Was this the last time that he tried to break in?"

"No," yesterday he tried one last time, but was driven away by security.

That doesn't sound too bad to me, it's not but I just wanted to let you know. I really appreciate that. But I need help getting the man's body out of the eel pond.

Hold on I'll be right back with something to help you, ten minutes later he came back with some rope and a winch.

Give me the rope, okay, Daten handed me pike the rope and he dropped the rope down into the eel pool and brought the dead body closer to him.

Mr. pike was able to get the rope around the dead man's arm, he pulled on the rope and pulled the dead man's body closer to the side of the eel pool. Don't just stare at the body, help me to get the body out of the pool.

Now give me the wench, so I can get his body the rest of the way out of the pool. Now let's pull his body out, it's so hard to move his body.

Stop complaining so much, it's true his body is so heavy and I can barely move it. I know it's so heavy but you don't hear me complaining do you.

No, I don't, but I'm going to keep pulling on his body until we can get it out. Alright now we got his body out

"How are you feeling?"

"I'm out of breath"

"How could that be?"

That was a lot of work, you know I'm twice as old as you are. I didn't even break a sweat; I have heard enough trash talk from you. Now since we got the body out of the eel pool

"What would you like to do next with body?"

"I guess just call the coroner and let him know that we have a body here for him to pick up."

"I don't have the coroners number, do you?"

"Yes," I do

Let me turn on my phone and check in it for the number. Hold on one-minute Sir, alright I have it.

"Are you ready for it?"

"Yes," its, 717-457-8875.

"Thank you, okay I got it."

Just give me a minute and I'll talk to you again soon. Mr. pike dialed the number and a man picked up.

"What do you need?"

"I have a dead body that needs to be picked up."

We will send someone out within the hour, okay have a good day and someone is going to pick up the body. Bye now.

"What did he say?"

"He said that he'll send someone out."

"How soon is he going to do that?"

"He said in an hour."

That's great, now how about you and I go write down about what happened today. You know I feel so bad about what happened to this poor guy. The guy was being mean to me and he got what was coming to him, you're such a cold-hearted guy.

"You have no sympathy for this guy, and what did he do to you?"

"He tried to push me into the eel pool with him."

That was wrong but he did nothing else to you. He yelled at me and gave me a hard time. Let's stop talking about the poor dead man. I hope he was a Christian and that he knew that God loved him.

"Are you a religious nut?"

"No," I'm not.

Chapter 4: Deterioration

I just believe that God loves me so. I don't know if God loves you, you did a bad deed letting him fall into the eel pool.

I told him not to move when he had fallen in the eel pool. He didn't listen to me and moved and the eels grabbed a hold of him and tore him up until he died. Let's stop discussing things that are religion based.

"What are you an Atheist?"

"No," I believe in God and don't ever call me an atheist again.

"Is that clear?"

"An hour later the coroner showed up at the gate."

The security guard dialed Mr. pike's walkie talkie number and asked him if it was alright to let the coroner into the lab.

Yes, Sir let him in now, alright will do, the coroner came in and had a mad look on his face. This is the first time that there was a bad accident at this facility.

"What do you people do at this facility?"

"Actually, we aren't able to tell you that"

"What's so secretive?"

You don't understand Sir, just take the body, and try not to ask me too many questions. Sir I could lose my job and so could Daten here.

 If I told you what we were doing here. I understand, I saw a sign somewhere around here that was talking about eel experiments.

I just wanted to know if you experimented with eels. Yes, we do and that's all that I'm going to say and willing to say.

> "How did this man die?"

> "I don't know you're the coroner. Can't you just look at the body and know what happened?"

> "No," I can't always do that

> "Did he fall or something?"

> "Yes," he fell down into the pool with the eels in it.

> "Why's he missing a body part?"

> "Did the eels do that to him?"

> "Yes," they did.

You know what sir this facility needs to be closed down, there's not much good happening anymore around here.

> "What do you mean?"

"The scientists aren't treating the eels with respect and they are dying. That's ashame, I hope that things get better around here."

"What's that smell?"

"I don't know Sir"

"What's it smell like?"

"It smells like chard metal or something like that."

I don't know where that smell could be coming from, it smells like it's coming out from below the floor.

The trouble is we are like fifty feet down beneath the water in this facility. Suddenly Mr. Pikes walkie talkie went off and someone began to yell.

Help us, help who. Blane just accidentally spilled a vile of growth hormone and it fell into the one eel pool.

One of the eels began to grow uncontrolledly and caused the pool eel pool to burst. There's water all over the floor, it's beginning to flood, we need to evacuate, this facility right now. There's a fire that started besides the burst eel pool.

"What should we do?"

"Get out of there and I'll then go on damage control I guess of the facility."

"Where's the one giant eel?"

"We don't know, it escaped and is now swimming through the bay."

"How big is it?"

"It's bigger than a man, soon it'll be as big as house."

"How are we going to stop it?"

"Do you guys have any ideas what to do?"

"No," we don't.

You know what I should do I should fire everyone and close down this facility. We're sorry for what happened, nobody around here seems to care. Now we have a serious problem, I'm more than mad at everyone.

"Are you mad at me?"

"No," I'm not mad at you.

My chest is beginning to feel like it's stiffening up and I feel like I can't breathe, help me.

"What do you want me to do?"

"I want you to hit on my chest to see if my heart will calm down."

I'm going to call 911, the coroner was looking at Mr. Pike, don't die on me. I don't want to have to drag you out of here too. Please hang on, don't go.

Alright my heart is feeling better, oh thank goodness. I hope I'll be okay. I think I'm still calling to call 911 for you. No, the EMTs won't come here, I have to leave the building before they can come.

That's not right, it's their rules not mine. Come on let's get out of here, so we can have you looked at by an EMT. Don't worry about the facility, everything is gone and we can't be wasting time getting out of here.

Our lives are more important than the condition that this facility stays in. Who cares if this whole facility falls apart and ends up in the bay, the eels don't care about you.

"So why are you so worried about them?"

"In case you haven't noticed Daten, it's my neck on the line if this secret experimental eel gets out and is spotted by the public."

I can get prosecuted for that and or thrown in jail for the rest of my life. The secret government is so strict and you wouldn't understand everything that I had to go through just to become a boss of this company. I had to go through secret briefings and the FBI was always looking over my shoulder and the CIA was also breathing down my back. Since the facility is going to be destroyed I'm going to have to pay for half of what the facility is worth to the secret government or they could look for me and have me killed.

I can't believe all the none sense that you're telling me, I don't believe half of what you just told me. For your information I don't care.

> "Then why should I help you get out of this sinking facility?"

> "It's the right thing to do, maybe I don't want to do the right thing this time and let you perish in this pathetic sinking facility."

I see how it is. Bye, I'm leaving now along with the coroner.

The facility began to quickly fill up with water and the water was now up to Mr. Pikes calves. Mr. Pike couldn't believe how quickly the water was coming in and the water was cold and made him begin to shake. He had goose bumps all the way down his back.

He was feeling like he was having difficulty breathing, like he couldn't catch his breath. The water was now up to his thighs.

Chapter 5: Observation

Mr. Pike could no longer stand and collapsed and his head was now submerged. He passed out and water was now going into his lungs filling them up.

He stopped breathing in a matter of minutes. Daten and the coroner were the only ones who survived the mishap at the secret facility.

Once Daten was safely out of the facility, he watched for an hour as the whole facility sank into the man-made bay. He got in his car and drove off and so did the coroner. Once he got home he took a nap and never thought about Mr. Pike again.

A few minutes later a colossal eel, came bursting up out of the bay. It saw all the dead bodies and quickly ate them up. After eating he grew 4 legs and walked along looking for more to eat.

The eel left out a loud screeching sound, thousands of salamanders came out of the swamp and surrounded him.

Together they searched for more prey, nearby there was a hunter looking for an alligator to shoot.

He was wading through the swamp, there were many mosquitoes buzzing around him. He heard something and crouched down

He looked through the rifles scope but didn't see anything. He heard a strange sound and hid behind a tree.

He got tired of waiting for whatever it was that made the sound and continued exploring the swamp.

He soon came to an abandoned boat, and carefully climbed into it. There was a tarp covering part of the back of the boat, his curiosity got the best of him and he lifted it up.

There was a carcass of a deer, many snakes came out of the body. This scared him so bad that he frantically tried to get out of the boat causing it to capsize.

Him and his gun were thrown into the swamp, one of the snakes were still after him. He grabbed a stick and wacked the snake in the head, but it only stunned it.

The snake tried to strike at his arm, and he hit it with the stick again finally killing it. He stood perfectly still, while a giant python crawled past him.

It could smell his scent in a boat and began to attack the boat. The smaller snakes felt threatened and went after it, but they were no match for the giant snakes strong jaws. It ate them all up, then it devoured the rest of the deer carcass.

The hunter was desperately searching through the swamp for his rifle, but still wasn't able to find it. He began searching through the swamp grass and was hoping to find it there.

Eventually he came across it, there was some mud and grass on it. He wiped the mud off of it with his glove, he looked over and the giant python was still attacking the boat.

When he saw that he took off through the swamp, he kept on going until he reached the boat launch.

He got into his truck and put his rifle on the passenger seat. He took off down the country road, and never looked back.

The Giant eel and the salamanders came to an alligator nesting ground. They found themselves in a fight with a giant alligator, the eel left out a massive shock that electrocuted the alligator to death.

Then it began to feed on the alligator, another smaller alligator was slowly approaching the eel. It charged the alligator and slammed into it with tremendous force killing it. Meanwhile a team of biologists were flying there observation drone, over a swamp looking for a particular species of frogs.

They observed many birds, and flying insects. The eel could sense that something was in the area and stopped feeding on the alligator.

The eel somehow made a huge shockwave, that traveled a long distance. The wave struck the drone, causing it to crash into the swamp. The biologists lost contact with the drone.

One of the biologists in the group suggested that they should go out and check things out. I don't think our boss would allow us to do that, besides that we don't get out of this office enough. We'll have a good time at the swamp, just don't forget your bug spray.

"Were you able to write down the drones location before we lost signal?"

"Yes," I was.

I know you aren't such a good driver so I'll drive. Grab your backpack and let's go, time is valuable here. I'm thinking that the drone should be 5 miles away from here, they all climbed into the suv and they took off.

You're going too fast, don't tell me how to drive. The police don't normally hangout along this road. If we don't get there quick enough someone else may find the drone first.

Watch out for that alligator if you hit one your truck is going to be ruined. They finally reached where they thought it was and pulled over the Suv. We're going to walk from here now, it shouldn't be a very long walk.

"Do you think there are many snakes in this swamp?"

"Yes," I'm sure there are.

I'm not wearing waders like you are, so my legs are going to be exposed. Just get over it and come over here, or I'm going to leave you behind.

Don't just look right in front of you, take a good look around you may see some wildlife. Look over at him, he's staring into his phone.

Then you should tell him to get off of his phone. That would just be a waste of my time, and energy. He might walk into an alligator, or trip over something.

Don't you worry yourself about him, he's on his own. The leader of the group found the drone in some tall grass.

"What's the condition of the drone?"

"It's in fair condition."

I don't know what you're talking about but it looks worse than that, one of the blades are broken. I can fix this drone tonight; I have extra parts for it. I ordered the parts off the internet a year ago, my order came in two days.

Suddenly they heard a loud shrieking sound, I don't want to know what that was. We should get back to the suv now, I'd like to see what it is. You can stay here and wait for it if it even comes at all.

The eel felt threatened by their presence and came out of the swamp and charged after them. It released its shocking energy, and it caused everyone to feel fatigued.

Step on it, the creature is coming. That creature is far too big, to be fast. I've got such a splitting headache, I'm not even sure what that creature resembled. I think that it looked like a giant snake, those creatures that surrounded the giant creature we're definitely salamanders.

I've never seen so many of them in one place, me neither. Those salamanders were a strange color, maybe it's just a new species. We should figure out a way to study them, you could fly over them with your drone.

Chapter 6: Thoughts

They might attack my drone, not if you keep it up high enough in the air. You haven't asked me what kind of creature I thought it could be. I think that it's an eel, but I've never seen an eel with legs.

We shouldn't tell our boss about this; he may fire us. I don't think so I think he'd be very interested in what we saw.

"Where did you get that book from?"

"From the center console."

It's a book about reptiles, and other water dwelling animals. Right now, I'm reading about the different species of salamanders, my favorite salamander is a giant salamander that lives in China.

"Are there any species of salamander that are venomous?"

"No," I don't think so.

We need to capture one of those salamanders that we saw, that's a good idea but don't expect me to assist you with that.

That eel had a large enough mouth to swallow a human, I'm afraid that thing is going to find its way into the city.

Don't dwell on that thing, think about what you're going to do back at the office. When we get back I'm going to make some coffee for all of us. You normally don't get tired during the day while you're working here.

That's because I had a very long night, let me guess you were at the bar again. Then you were at a party, no I was just at a friend's house.

"Isn't he a heavy smoker"

"Yes," he is.

"Doesn't that bother you, no it don't."

"Did you have any beers at his place?"

"No," I just had some water.

It sounds to me, you're on the wagon. Getting drunk anymore just isn't any fun anymore. I've gained a lot of weight from drinking beer, and no I'm not on a diet.

He parked the vehicle and they got out and entered their office. Careful you don't drop the drone; I carry it like this all of the time. I think that we should each buy a drone for ourselves.

I thought that they were very expensive, it depends on the kind and quality that you get. I would buy just a typical camera drone, and some extra batteries for it.

Because the batteries in these things don't last very long. I think I should give my friend in the national guard a call about the giant eel, I wouldn't do that.

He probably won't even believe you when you tell him about it. Hopefully that eel will find its way back to the ocean and just swim away.

I think that the eel isn't going to the ocean. I believe that the eel is hungry, he's looking around for food.

"What are you typing in your laptop?"

"What I got done today."

I write a little bit about what I do here every day, I don't think that's warranted. I showed it to my boss before, he said I should keep it up.

I'd like to know how long a salamander lives for, that's easy several years. The neighbors kid used to have a pet salamander, he even named it.

The pet that I had when I was a kid was a gerbil, and I couldn't stand that thing. So, I gave to my sister, I doubt that she kept it either.

I didn't have an animal when I was growing up, you say that with such a sad look on your face. I used to play in the sandbox a lot, to this day I still like to go to the beach. I haven't been to the beach in for so long.

The ground below them began to shake, they looked out the window and saw the giant eel and the salamanders.

Several police cars pulled up in front of the creatures, the salamanders had grown from just seeing them earlier.

There were four officers shooting at the salamanders, and eel. The salamanders were spitting some kind of substance at the officers, one of the officers collapsed while the other officers ran back to their cars. There probably calling for backup right now, I'm glad that they stopped shooting at them. I'm surprised that none of the creatures, fell over from getting shot so many times.

It's like their bodies instantly heal up after getting shot, I never saw such a thing before. Maybe if we got some of their genes we could use them to help cure people of diseases.

After what just happened with the officers those things are dangerous. I don't even think we'll be safe in this place for very long.

We should be just fine in this place; I don't think those things are smart enough to figure out that were in here.

I disagree about them not being smart, they're smarter than you give them credit for. I'm sure that the National Guard will be on their way shortly, I wonder what'll stop those things, an army tank.

Something that'll blow them apart. Quit talking so much, we have to find a way out of here. I tried to open the back door but it wouldn't open, it does tend to get stuck sometimes. I'm sure if you give it a good kick it will open up, he gave it a good kick but it didn't budge.

"Do you have any other ideas?"

"No," not at the moment.

Another person in the group took the fire extinguisher off the wall and began ramming it into the front door. This didn't seem to help either, with anger he slammed the fire extinguisher down on the floor. I haven't seen you that angry in a long time, I just want to get out of here, we do too.

All of us need to come together here. Whatever you do stay away from that window, the giant eel is looking in the window. I'm not afraid of that thing looking at me, I'd like to fight that thing.

There's no way that you could win against that thing, it would gobble you up very quickly. I'd cut up, its insides until it spit me out again.

The eel slammed down onto the building with all its weight, it left out a screeching sound and left off a massive shock.

The shock was so powerful, that it electrocuted all the men to death. The salamanders found their way into the building, through the collapsed roof.

The salamanders smelled their bodies, and a strange reaction went through their bodies turning them into carnivores. They quickly devoured the bodies and joined back with the eel.

A woman was driving down the street when she saw the giant eel and the salamanders. She immediately did a U-turn and took off the other way. Further down the road, she pulled over.

She took her phone out of her pocket and began texting her friends. You won't believe what I just saw, she even texted her boyfriend.

Several dogs had gotten loose and went running down the street. The minute that they saw the giant eel and the salamanders, they began barking. The salamanders lurched forward, then the dogs ran off.

Chapter 7: Fierce Battle

One of the salamanders gave chase after one of the dogs, it caught up to the dog and killed it with a swift blow to the head.

A man saw the creatures, and quickly ran to his truck to get his gun. After grabbing his gun, he began firing at all the creatures. He shot one of the salamanders many times, and it collapsed.

He soon ran out of ammunition and retreated back into his home. He searched through his living room for some more ammunition but couldn't find any.

He called his son asking him if he had any more ammunition, but he said that he had just shot his last bullet. After hanging up with his son, he went over to the refrigerator and pulled out a piece of pizza from the prior evening.

He got a paper plate out of the kitchen cabinet and placed it on the table. He put the piece of pizza down on it, got up again and got himself a beer.

He forgot that he had let the side window down, the salamanders could smell him and began searching around the house for a way to get in. One of them spotted the open window and shoved his head through it.

But he pushed forward and broke through the window. The man heard the glass breaking, and immediately walked into his living room. He grabbed the samurai sword, off the shelf, firmly holding it in his hand.

The salamander came angrily charging down the hall towards him, he took a swing at it, but it dodged the sword. Before he had a minute to react, it forcibly slammed him into the wall.

The salamander chose not to devour him and wondered into the kitchen. It could smell something; it hadn't smelled before. It got up on the table and feasted on the pizza. After it was done eating, it found its way back outside through the kitchen window.

Some stray cats came out of an old shed nearby to see what was going on. The salamander heard them and chased after them, one of the cats tripped and it grabbed the cat. The cat tried to escape but the salamander bit into it, killing it.

An elderly woman was planting plants in her garden, when she saw the salamander walking down the street. She stopped what she was doing and retreated inside when she saw it.

It could smell her sent in the garden and began tearing it apart. She couldn't bare to watch it destroying her garden and looked away. She went back into a backroom and came back out with a taser and a pistol.

She turned on the taser, and quickly opened the door and threw the taser at the salamander. It crushed the tazor and smashed through her picket fence and was now in the neighbor's yard.

There was a dog sitting on a chair looking out the bay window. After seeing the salamander, it curled up and got away from the window. The grandmother went outside holding her gun, looking for the salamander but didn't see it and returned to sitting on the couch.

The lone salamander joined back up with the others, they kept on destroying properties and killing. A retired marine and a firemen, teamed up together and went after the creatures with assault rifles and fireworks.

They went after the salamanders with all they had, shooting at them relentlessly. It only infuriated the salamanders, causing them to be more violent. They spite out poison at the men when it touched there skin it burned.

The eel left out a massive shock, that electrocuted the men to death. The military sent out men to fight the eel and salamanders, sometime later they didn't return to the base.

Later that evening, a race of aliens were having a meeting about the extermination of dangerous creatures on and beyond their planet.

They had already killed 5 deadly creatures. After the meeting was over, the aliens sent out there spy drone that went to Earth.

Sometime later the drone entered the Earth's atmosphere and kept flying until they could see what was on the ground.

They came up on a highly populated city and didn't stop until they came to a less populated residential area.

Then they spotted the creatures, who were fighting with humans in the street. When the people saw the drone they took cover.

They quickly programmed the distance of the creatures from the coordinates that they got from the drone into the galactic incinerating laser.

It took a moment for the laser to warm up, then it fired the explosive incinerating beam at the target.

The laser had hit the eel on its side, causing it to collapse. All of the salamanders, accept one ran off towards the woods, not to be seen again.